ESCAPE FROM THE WORKHOUSE

About the Author

Patricia Barnard was born in the Fens and now lives with her husand in a Cambridgeshire village. Apart from writing for children she writes articles, plays and poetry. She enjoys theatre, cottage gardening and dabbling unsuccessfully in arts and crafts. Forced onto a desert island she would take the Bible, Shakespeare, *Finnegans Wake*, the poetry of John Clare and a cabin trunk full of the absorbing memorabilia of the years spent bringing up a family of five.

ESCAPE FROM THE WORKHOUSE

Adventure in Victorian Cambridge

by Patricia Barnard

Anglia Young Books

First published in 1989
by Anglia Young Books
Durhams Farmhouse, Ickleton
Saffron Walden, Essex CB10 1SR

Reprinted 1993

Illustrations by Tessa Hamilton

Design and production in association with
Book Production Consultants
47 Norfolk Street
Cambridge CB1 2LE

British Library Cataloguing in Publication Data
Barnard, Patricia
  Escape from the workhouse.
  I. Title
  823'.914 [J]

ISBN 1-871173-03-5

Typeset in 11/15 point Palatino by Witwell Ltd, Southport
and printed in Great Britain by
Redwood Books

AUTHOR'S NOTE

Most of the action of this story takes place on a Monday, Tuesday and Wednesday in October 1843.

• • • • •

The author wishes to acknowledge the kind help given by Mr Mike Petty and staff at the Cambridgeshire Collection in the Central Library, Lion Yard, Cambridge in making available maps, newspapers and documents relating to the period covered by this story.

CHAPTER ONE

'I've got to get out of here!' Colley muttered in the darkness of the blank walled dormitory as he listened to the uneasy breathing of the boys sleeping in rows on either side of him. Like him, they were orphans, or the children of paupers or criminals, forced to live the grim life of the workhouse through no fault of their own.

Colley was worn out, but he couldn't sleep. His small, thin body tossed under the rough grey blanket. He thought of his loving parents and his father's chandler's shop in Trinity Street. He tried to remember the ox-tallow smell of the basement room where the pale yellow candles hung in rows. That life changed for ever two years ago when both his parents died of typhoid fever and strangers had hurried him away from them.

He remembered being brought to the workhouse. It was his ninth birthday. He had always been called Colley, but then stern voices called out his full name "Nicholas Dawkin" and he went to the icy washhouse with the other pale, unsmiling children who had arrived with him.

For a time he had marched to school in the heavy

grey clothes given to him. 'There go the workhouse children,' people said.

'You're lucky to have this roof over your head,' he had been told. He knew from Jock, his pauper friend, who had tramped the roads, that some children slept under hedges, even in winter, and everywhere children of the poor worked in factories, mines and fields to help to keep their families alive.

Colley buried his face and banged his fist onto the hard mattress. 'I *will* get away!'

The next evening in the recreation hour, Jock said 'The Queen is coming to Cambridge. Prince Albert too. There'll be fireworks for us on Parker's Piece. I'd like to see the Queen, God bless her, but she won't be coming round here. She doesn't know what it's like for us.'

'I must get away from here!' Colley said, when the other boys had moved away. He said it desperately and stared up into the lined face of the old pauper who sat beside him on the rough wooden bench.

'Aye, Colley, my lad, we'd all like to get out of this place.'

'I'm going to run away!'

'You'd be brought back,' said Jock, drawing slowly at the dregs of his precious tobacco.

This was the only free hour in the long working day. Jock had no right to be in the boys' recreation room, smoking his pipe, but he went there to escape the shrieks of the mad inmates.

'Will you help me, Jock – please?' asked Colley. Jock silently puffed at his pipe. Colley looked at the other boys. They were too tired to play. They leaned listlessly on the scrubbed table, or turned the pages of old almanacks. Some idly rolled marbles on the cold floor.

Suddenly a boy burst into the room:
'The charity people have been! They've taken Alfie! The sweep's got him!'

They all knew what that meant. Colley thought of Alfie, choked with soot, climbing and clinging to hot chimney bricks. Charities paid the premiums for the boys and the workhouse willingly let them go. Which of them would be next? In the silence that followed Colley fixed his eyes on Jock. Jock came out of his long reverie.

'You can't walk out through the gates, or climb the railings. Someone would see you,' warned Jock.

'Then I'll go at night!'

'You can't do that. That iron gate across your stairs is locked at night. I've seen them doing it. God help you all if there's a fire.'

'It's the locks I can't stand,' said Colley, despairingly.

'There *is* a way,' said Jock in a low voice, 'but don't tell anyone it was my idea.'

'I won't' said Colley, eagerly. 'What is it?'

'You *could* escape in the miller's cart, hiding under the sacks.'

'Oh yes!' cried Colley, and then he became aware of a sudden silence in the room, as though the word "escape" had penetrated into the numbed minds of all the boys. Then a boy with a mouth organ began to draw harsh tuneless sounds from it.

'But how can I get into the goods yard where the cart comes?' asked Colley.

'Ask if you can work in the bakehouse.'

'I will!' Colley smiled at the old man. 'Thanks Jock.'

'Go as far as the cart goes. That'll be to the mill at Newnham. Then run for your life boy!'

Colley asked the master of the workhouse for permission to work in the bakehouse and after a time he was sent there. He soon learned the workings of it. He staggered in with slopping buckets of water from the yard pump; he scrubbed the flagged floor and cleaned the huge dough troughs. He also learned which days the miller's cart came.

'It's to-morrow, Jock – Monday' he whispered, as Jock hobbled past into the men's exercise yard.

The next day the miller's cart rumbled into the yard. The miller's man jumped down and began unloading the full sacks of flour. The horse stood patiently snorting into his empty raffia nose-bag. Colley waited, shivering with fear and excitement.

Colley's job was to take out the empty sacks from the last delivery. He piled them up in the cart. At last he threw in the last sack. The moment had come!

In a flash, as the miller's man lingered in the bakehouse, Colley leapt over the dropped tailboard and crawled under the dusty sacks. He held his breath as he heard the miller's man returning. The tailboard was clamped shut.

The horse moved off, clattering the traces and jangling the harness. The whip lashed the air and the cart began to rock violently. Colley's head bumped up and down on the hard floor. His elbows knocked against the bruising wood as the cart jolted over the rough stony road. He hardly dared to think about the bakehouse.

They would be looking for him and if he was found, he'd be sent to the Punishment Room. Boys sent to the Punishment Room had to wear special clothes so that everyone knew they were in disgrace.

The huge wooden wheels rolled along beside Parker's Piece, past the forbidding New Gaol, across Regent Street, down Crab Lane and into Trumpington Street. There Colley heard a hubbub of people jostling on the cobbles. He moved the sacks from one eye. He saw evergreens, flowers and banners. "Welcome your Majesty!" he read. So Jock was right. The Queen *was* coming.

Colley knew by the strong river smell and the shouts of the bargees that he was crossing the Cam. College washing flapped on Laundress Green, the weir roared and he knew that soon he must jump.

'Whoa!' cried the miller's man, but before the wheels came to a standstill Colley leapt over the endboard and ran blindly across the fen.

CHAPTER TWO

Colley dashed across a plank bridge onto the green and into a noisy crowd of bargees and millworkers coming out of the taverns in Mill Lane. They stared at the small white figure with flour and dust flying from his bakehouse smock as he ran.

Then he felt a heavy hand on his shoulder and heard a slurred voice: 'Not so fast, lad. Look where you're going.'

Colley wriggled free and dashed through Laundress Lane into Silver Street. Dodging the horse traffic, he crossed the road and plunged into some evergreen bushes on the river bank opposite Queens' College. There he crouched, panting for breath.

He felt almost part of the green bush as sharp dead twigs pricked him and strange smelling leaves brushed his face. He took off his bakehouse smock and hid it in the bush. Then he parted the leaves and peeped through.

The bargees were noisily tying up their barges to huge rings projecting from college walls that were half submerged in the water. As they waited to unload corn, coal or rushes the men could jump from barge to barge, so closely packed was the river traffic.

Then, almost beside Colley's hiding place, two young men in long black gowns and black tasselled caps, greeted each other.

'Sebastian, what's this jape I hear you are plotting?' asked one of them.

'It's a treasure hunt to celebrate this grand visit,' answered Sebastian. 'The poor scholars can look for the treasure. Look at that dilapidated creature,' he added languidly.

They both looked, and Colley looked too. A young scholar leaned on the bridge. Shreds hung from his gown and his coat and trousers were shabby and faded.

'I haven't decided what to hide yet.' Sebastian said. His friend laughed and they set off in different directions.

Impulsively Colley decided to follow Sebastian. He would lose himself in the crowds in the town. He followed Sebastian across the bridge, past the impoverished scholar, across courtyards and out into the lane in front of the college. Facing him were some ramshackle cottages where shawled women clustered round a pump, clanging their pails and talking loudly so as to be heard over the constant noise of cart wheels and the hobnailed clopping of horses' hooves on the flinted and cobbled streets.

Sebastian Snode made his way gingerly into the noise and stench of Cambridge. He walked quickly, his nose rather high in the air, and almost fell over some small boys playing on the pavement. Carefully removing the folds of his gown from the grimy urchin who had been swept into it, he noticed that the boys had been playing with coloured marbles. 'The very thing,' thought Sebastian. The surprised little gang gawped up at him open-mouthed but silent, their game suspended by this unexpected encounter.

'I will buy your marbles,' Sebastian told them, 'for a shilling.'

The bargain was immediately struck by a nodding of heads. The money was seized and the children fled, leaving Sebastian Snode to lower himself to the pavement to pick up the marbles of many colours. 'Perfect,' thought Sebastian and smiled to himself.

Colley waited and watched. It was two years since he had walked about freely or played a game and he began to experience a forgotton feeling. He was enjoying himself.

Sebastian started to hide the marbles. He hurried along King's Parade and Colley scurried after him as Sebastian disappeared into Senate House Lane. He hid marbles behind gilded coats of arms, and in a wall blackened with age he found a hole left by decaying mortar. In went a black marble. Round the corner he almost bumped into Colley as they got mixed up with an unruly crowd pushing and struggling to get into the Senate House to see the royal preparations. Colley was swept up the gallery stairs. He could hardly see over the balcony. He was forced down against a crowd trying to get up the stairs. He hurried after Sebastian across King's Parade and watched as Sebastian slipped a marble between the hard petals of an iron lily in the railings of St. Mary's church.

Cambridge was in a bustling ferment, bubbling with anticipation like a great civic pot coming up to the boil. Everything that went on wheels was out in the streets – wagons, carts, drays, coaches, carriages, hand carts, dog carts and wheelbarrows – as well as solitary horsemen and carefree dogs. Children were out bowling hoops along the uneven pavements. One swept past Colley and he longed to seize the stick and chase it. In Bene't Street Colley and Sebastian leapt aside as a coach and four swept into the courtyard of the Eagle Inn.

At Peas Hill it was not the day for the fishmarket but the smell lingered there, staking out its claim for the next market. Sebastian paused at the entrance to the town centre. He had never ventured there before. He looked at the huddled conglomeration of houses that almost filled the centre, their little yards backing onto the great church. Pump Lane divided them from other rows of houses.

Sebastian picked his way down the dirty streets pinching his delicate nostrils together. The over-powering smell from the malting houses and breweries and the heavy smell of goats' skins from the cordwainers' yards were added to the permanent aroma of drains, horses and warm, rubbed leather. He hurried along Pump Lane. Suddenly a high lattice window was flung open and a voice called "Heads!" He did not look up. Down came the contents of a pail, narrowly missing him. Colley, not far behind, found himself laughing, but not out loud. He had almost forgotten how to laugh.

Sebastian sped on, past rows of poor dwellings, black smoke from their chimneys swirling around him.

'A tinder box,' he thought fearfully. 'One spark and they will devour each other.'

He arrived, with Colley following, at the narrow L-shaped strip that was the market place. Women with wooden yokes on their shoulders filled buckets with water from the conduit at the corner of Petty Cury and clanked away over the cobbles. Sebastian hid a marble on the conduit.

Colley feasted his eyes on the fruit stalls. They were

crowded and as untidy as a burst pomegranate. In the Shambles he saw Sebastian wedging a marble into one of the wooden posts of a stall.

The Mayor, Aldermen and Burgesses hurried into the ancient Guildhall, muttering in nervous rehearsal the lines they would have to speak before the Queen. Colley was so engrossed in watching soldiers marching past that he lost sight of Sebastian. Then he saw him lingering uneasily at the entrance to Petty Cury.

'One marble each,' decided Sebastian, 'for the Red Lion, the Red Hart, the Wrestlers and the Antelope.' Colley went after him into the stable yards behind the inns, dodging through the market traders' carts crowded there. Sebastian avoided Falcon Yard. He had been told of "steaming, reeking mounds of slops and dung" there. He hurried out into Petty Cury again, only to find himself engulfed in a crowd that surged towards him in the wake of some carriages.

'Her Majesty's dresses are in that one,' shouted an excited voice.

'Twelve servants have arrived at the Red Lion to look after them,' called another. Strangers began to speak to each other.

As Sebastian battled his way against the crowds, Colley followed. Suddenly the large shadow of a constable appeared amongst the carts. In a panic Colley ran out and plunged into Falcon Yard. He dashed behind some barrels and hid there.

By now Sebastian had reached Free School Lane. He turned into the University Botanic Garden, relieved to be away from the pungent town. Back in the college grounds he hid the last marble in some ivy. Then he scrawled a notice and hung it on the cloister wall:

"POOR SCHOLARS. CALL AT ROOM 2 STAIRCASE Q. YOU WILL LEARN SOMETHING TO YOUR ADVANTAGE."

In Falcon Yard Colley's senses were almost over-powered by the sewage and filth around him. He had lost Sebastian. The game of hiding marbles was over and he remembered, his fears returning, that he was running away. He heard the constable coming into the yard. Then came the loud knocking which shook the ramshackle doors. Old crones opened their doors a crack. Colley's heart was thumping as he thought of being caught by the constable and returned to the punishment waiting for him in the workhouse. Time stood still. Then, at last, the police boots marched away.

CHAPTER THREE

Colley stood up. He had noticed a grating beside a barrel and now from the broken window behind it the inviting smell of cooking came slinking through the bars, driving out even the vile smells around him. Colley leant over to breathe it in. Suddenly the face of an old woman, more ravaged than the faces he had seen in the workhouse, looked up at him from behind the grating.

'Want something to eat?' she asked. She had seen his thin legs and his workhouse boots. Colley was taken off guard but quickly recovered himself. He was hungry.

'Please,' he said. The woman came up and opened the door and Colley followed her down the narrow, rickety stairs into the dark, grimy basement. The old woman pushed a chipped bowl of brown liquid towards Colley and he sat down on a box covered with a sack. She pottered round the miserable room, muttering to herself:

'All this fuss about the Queen's visit. What's it to us? The constable has been here. He got nothing from me. I'll tell you something no-one else knows. The men here are whispering about something.'

'What about?' Colley asked, his eyes wide, over the top of his bowl.

'A surprise for the Queen. You wait and see.'

'What sort of surprise?' Colley persisted.

'A nasty one, I should think.'

The old woman cackled with laughter at the thought of it. She suddenly seemed to Colley more like a hideous hag than the kindly soul he had taken her for. He got up quickly and calling his thanks he dashed up the stairs. At the top the doorway went dark. His way was barred by a huge, bearded man. He grasped Colley's closely cropped head:
'What's the hurry? What have you been up to down there?' His voice was ugly and threatening. Colley reacted quickly. With a few nimble twists of his body he was free. He ran into the crowds in Petty Cury. He must get away into the countryside where he could hide.

He darted into Slaughterhouse Lane as a herd of bullocks came pushing and shoving towards him, urged on by sticks and shouts. He flattened himself against the wall as they came, caked with dried mud, stumbling against him and mooing poignantly as though they knew what waited for them in the slaughterhouse.

At last he was free of the town and running towards

the fen. It was getting dark. He stopped running when he came to the walled garden of an old house. The house looked lonely and forlorn in the twilight.

'I'll hide here,' he decided, 'in one of those outhouses.' He climbed through a hole in the wall and went past the back of the rambling house. As he passed the window he saw a pale, curly haired boy deeply absorbed in writing at a table lit by an oil lamp. He crept pas keeping low. Some stone steps led down to a heavy oak door. There was a small unglazed window. As he drew level with it, a door in the house opened.

Desperate not to be found, Colley dived through the little window, somersaulted and landed on his feet a long way down in a cavernous cellar. Footsteps came and went. A door closed again and he was alone in the musty darkness of the cellar. He tried the heavy door but it was locked on the outside. As his eyes grew used to the darkness, he saw gnawed holes in the apples spread out on the stone floor. He knew what that meant and he stood still, listening. Yes, there they were. Rats stumbled and blundered over the apples, their small eyes gleaming. Colley stood rigidly, hardly daring to breathe, as they came closer and closer and lumbered over his boots, their tails trailing after them like living bootlaces. At last they slithered away into their secret places.

Colley moved cautiously. He found another flight of

stone steps leading up to the house. He climbed them and tried the door at the top but this was also locked. Colley pressed his ear to the door, but no sounds came from the house.

He looked up at the huge oak beams that supported the old floorboards of the room above. Suddenly heavy footsteps made the floorboards shake. Wood-wormed dust sprinkled down onto Colley's upturned face. Then he heard voices clearly.

'Well, Douglas?' boomed a man's voice. 'How far have you got with your route map of the Queen's journey?'

'As far as Waltham Cross, Papa,' came from the boy.

'They'll put in a new relay of horses there at the New Inn. Then again at the Bull at Ware. You can work out how many horses will pull the Queen's carriage to Cambridge, with four horses in harness.'

'I like it best when she goes from Slough to Paddington by the Great Western Railway,' said Douglas.

'Ah, yes, that's the future, my son. I'll warrant you that the next time Her Majesty comes to Cambridge she'll come all the way by train. Now that the railways have started, there'll be no stopping them.'

The floorboards rocked and shed centuries old dust as the father moved towards the door. Colley felt his way round the cellar. Where could he sleep and be safe from rats?

It was then that he found the secret tunnel. It was about four feet high and built of bricks. He peered into its arched darkness and heard water dripping through the old brickwork. He moved away from it, feeling his way round the cellar's cold walls. At last he felt some rough wood. A cupboard. he climbed into its filthy shelter and closed the door. He did not mind the darkness. It had been a friend, hiding his tears in his early days at the workhouse. But he couldn't sleep and already his imagination was groping for an answer to his problem. How was he to get out of the cellar? Would a pile of apples help him to reach the little window?

'To-morrow I'll find a way,' he vowed. 'I'll get out somehow.'

CHAPTER FOUR

On Tuesday morning Colley woke stiff and hungry. He crunched part of an apple. Then he tried to pile the apples up to stand on them, but when he climbed on them they collapsed, again and again. There was no way of reaching the high window. There was only one thing to do:

'Help!' he shouted again and again but no answer came.

At last he heard the boy in the garden calling the cat.

'Isambard! Isambard!'

Colley quickly picked up some of the apples and began to aim them at the little window. One of them sailed through.

Outside in the garden Douglas was alarmed. Who could possibly be hurling an apple out of the cellar window? Isambard shot up a tree and hung onto the bark, looking back over his shoulder balefully.

'Help!' called Colley again from the depths of the cellar. Douglas ran into the house and stood in the hall outside the cellar door.

'Who is it?' he asked nervously.

'Colley,' came the reply. Hearing a boy's voice re-assured Douglas a little. Nervously he turned the great rusty key and opened the door slightly. He peered down the steps to where Colley stood looking up at him. Colley's wild and extraordinary appearance, with cobwebs clinging to him, gave Douglas as much shock as though he had encountered a troglodyte who had lived in the cellar all his life. He gripped the door handle.

'What are you doing in the cellar?' he asked.

'I ran away from the workhouse. I got in through the window and slept in the cupboard.'

'You slept in the *cellar*!' repeated Douglas, amazed. He went down the steps.

'I'm very hungry,' said Colley.

'I'll get you something,' said Douglas. 'My father's out and Mrs Claxton's gone into town. She's our housekeeper.'

He fetched bread and a chicken leg. Colley gasped at the sight of it and immediately began to eat. He did not speak again until he had finished. Douglas watched, mesmerized by this strange boy who had appeared from nowhere.

'I can't go back to the workhouse. You won't tell, will you?'

'No, I won't tell,' Douglas promised. 'You can hide here if you like.'

'Thanks. Until they've forgotten about me.'

They both relaxed and sat down on the steps. Douglas closed the door behind them.

'I've never been down here before,' he confessed. 'I should be at school, but I've been ill with scarlet fever.'

'Oh,' said Colley. The word "fever" brought painful memories.

'To-morrow I'm riding with my father to Royston. There'll be hundreds of riders out there to bring the Queen and Prince Albert to Cambridge.'

'I shan't see the Queen,' said Colley wistfully.

'Did you know she's going from Slough to Paddington by train?'

'Yes, I heard you and your father talking through the floorboards.'

They laughed together in the gloom of the cellar.

'Guess who's driving the train?'

'I don't know.'

'Mr Brunel himself. Mr Isambard Kingdom Brunel.'

'Who's Mr Brunel?' asked Colley.

'A great engineer,' said Douglas enthusiastically.

'I'm going to be an engineer one day. Mr Brunel's the chief engineer for the Great Western Railway. My father says railways will be everywhere.'

'Perhaps I could work on them,' said Colley. 'But I'd like to go to school. I haven't been to school much. I never shall now.'

'They'll have to make railcoaches then, not stage coaches,' continued Douglas. 'Mr Brunel designs steamers and great bridges to hang over rivers and gorges. He's built a tunnel under the Thames lined with bricks.'

'Like the one over there,' said Colley.

There was a silence.

'Where? I've never seen it,' Douglas said slowly.

'Come and look!' urged Colley.

They made their way to the tunnel. It was hardly visible but it was outlined by the greater darkness inside. Timidly Douglas drew back:
'I don't like it,' he said.

'Where does it go to?' asked Colley.

'I don't know. Some people say it goes to the college, because this is called Old College House. No-one really knows.'

'It must go somewhere,' persisted Colley. 'Let's explore it.'

'No!' exclaimed Douglas with mounting anxiety. Colley looked at him sideways:
'You'll have to go down tunnels when you're an engineer like Mr Brunel,' he said.

Douglas wavered: 'All right,' he said at last. 'I suppose I shall. I'll get a light. But we mustn't be long because I'm going into Cambridge this morning with my cousin to see the decorations.'

He fetched a candle. Colley took it and went first into the tunnel. He hardly had to bend at all but Douglas had to stoop. They stumbled along the wet passageway, the candle throwing yellow light and horrid shadows on the ancient brickwork.

'Brunel's tunnel had a steel cover to keep the water out,' said Douglas, 'and then the bricks. This one only has brick. It doesn't look strong, the water's dripping in everywhere. It's horrible.' He was talking fast to hide his nervousness.

'Let's turn back,' he said.

'Just a bit further,' urged Colley.

They went slowly forward, getting more silent and chilled as they went deeper and deeper into the inhospitable passageway, absorbed now in the grim fascination of their adventure.

'Look!' said Douglas, taking the candle from Colley and holding it close to the arched roof. 'Those bricks are rotten. I'm going back.' He turned to go, but as he spoke there was a loud cracking sound. The bricks behind them gave way, followed by a cascade of rubble and earth. The tunnel behind them was blocked!

They did not know that overhead a heavy dray delivering coal into the coalhouse had been too much for the tunnel to bear. The heavy wheels had sunk into the drive, pressing the earth onto the rotten bricks making the tunnel collapse.

Douglas was frozen with fright. Colley went forward, only to find that at some date the tunnel had been bricked up, perhaps to prevent anyone from making his way down it and coming up in the cellar.

'We're trapped!' gasped Douglas. 'We'll never get out!'

'We will. We *must*,' said Colley grimly.

Then the candle went out.

CHAPTER FIVE

Neither of the boys spoke. Fear and panic gripped them. Douglas moved to grasp Colley's arm and heard the matches rattling in his pocket. With trembling hands he relit the candle. They began to shout, but Douglas was weak and his voice did not carry.

'It's no good,' said Douglas. 'We're too deeply in. No-one will hear us.' He tried to keep the terror out of his voice but failed. Colley knew that everything depended on him:
'Everyone will be out looking for you,' he said.

'But they won't look down here. They know I've never been near the cellar in my life.'

They fell silent, considering what that meant and sank down helplessly onto the wet rubble.

Suddenly Colley struggled to his feet.

'Air!' he said urgently. 'We must have air!'

He began with his strong hardworked hands to pull at the rubble and earth, feverishly clawing at the obstruction until his nails bled. At last he broke through. He stretched his thin arm through the hole he had made. His hand moved freely in the chill air beyond.

'Done it!' cried Colley.

'I don't know what I would have done without you,' said Douglas gratefully.

But as Colley tried to enlarge the airway more masonry crumbled down. As the dray and its four horses had made its heavy way down the drive, the sweep had arrived, with Alfie from the workhouse trudging miserably behind the cart, to sweep the great chimneys of Old College House. The cart's wheels had rolled into the unexpected dip and were bent and damaged. These new rumblings died away and there was silence in the tunnel, except for the slow dripping of water. The hours dragged by.

'We must keep awake, then we'll hear when they call. We must keep talking,' urged Colley.

'Tell me about the workhouse,' said Douglas.

'We had bread and gruel every morning. For supper we had bread and broth. We had rice pudding on Friday. Everything was runny ...'

'Is that why you ran away?' put in Douglas. They smiled feebly for the first time in their dark prison.

'At least the rats don't want to come in here with us,' said Colley.

'It was the rats and the dark I couldn't bear, and things I heard about a ghost haunting the tunnel. That's why I never went down.' Douglas shivered. 'I'm cold, are you?'

'Not too cold. The women in the workhouse sewed these strong clothes.'

'My aunt's on some committee that helps boys from the workhouse,' said Douglas.

'The charity people,' said Colley, grimly. 'They took Alfie. Don't tell your Aunt about me, will you?'

'Of course I won't,' said Douglas. 'I'll tell you about my cousin Louise. She lives with my aunt and uncle at Mulberry House in Trumpington Street. I was going over there this morning – was it this morning? I wonder what the time is?'

They became engrossed in their own thoughts.

'Do you know what a nit is?' Colley asked suddenly.

'No.'

'It's a louse's egg. They lay them in your hair. They make you want to scratch and scratch. At the workhouse they scraped our heads with sharp steel combs.'

'How horrible,' said Douglas. Colley began to scratch his short crop of hair. Douglas found himself doing the same thing through his long curls.

'When I had scarlet fever,' said Douglas, 'the skin came off everywhere. I kept some huge bits, but Mrs Claxton burnt them. The worst thing was she took my books and cooked them in the oven to kill the germs. They went brown. Robinson Crusoe was ruined.'

'I haven't got any books,' said Colley. 'But I can read. We read old almanacks or chronicles.'

'I've got some good fairy tales. They came from Germany. Awful things happen in them.'

'Worse than this?'

'Horrid, magic things. Like being turned into an animal and trapped for ever in its skin,' said Douglas.

'What would it be like to be turned into a rat?' wondered Colley.

To pass the time they thought how they would try to show people they were the missing boys, if they became rats. Colley would go back to the workhouse and run about in the bakehouse tearing at the sacks of flour. He would gnaw through into the recreation room and become a secret evening pet for the children.

But the idea of being rats soon seemed even more horrible than their present plight.

'I wonder what's going on outside?' said Douglas at

last. 'I expect Louise gave up waiting for me and went out.' They could think of no more to say and lapsed again into a despairing silence.

• • • • •

Meanwhile Cambridge was already in turmoil, and the people were further diverted by the sudden appearance of what seemed to be a pack of demented scholars in shabby gowns and battered untasselled caps. They were dashing around as though looking for something. They searched high and low, throwing themselves into the hunt with gusto. Stallholders were quite annoyed to see the swans and geese which lay in majestic feather on the rough trestle tables, being upturned and ruffled.

'Hi!' shouted a butcher at the Shambles as his hanging carcases were disturbed by a hand removing something from one of his stall posts. Then a shout of triumph drew the tattered pack to see what had been found.

'Get back to your books, idlers,' muttered the stallholders. The poor scholars, and some rich ones too wearing specially hired rags so that they could join in the hunt, rushed all over Cambridge. They got entangled with a flock of sheep peacefully passing Sidney Sussex College. Dogs barked delightedly at the excitement, lunged at the flying tatters and joined the chase.

Douglas had been missed as soon as Mrs. Claxton returned.

'I can't find Douglas,' she told his father anxiously. 'I've searched everywhere. He was to have ridden to Mulberry House but his pony is still in the field.'

They both searched again. Then Douglas's father decided to ride over to Mulberry House to see if Douglas had walked there. They did not search the cellar. They knew Douglas would never go down there.

CHAPTER SIX

As Douglas's father rode to Mulberry House, Louise was skipping happily along beside her governess, Miss Primty, sharing in the excitement in the town. The town crier in his brilliant scarlet robes and black buckled shoes was ringing his bell for attention. Louise peered in a shop window:

'French millinery,' she read. 'That's where Mama bought her blue feather snake.'

'Boa,' corrected Miss Primty.

'Look!' cried Louise as the raggle taggle group of scholars rushed past them and began climbing about the gateways of colleges.

'They seem to have lost something,' said Louise.

'They're always up to some caper,' said Miss Primty.

"Mind the ladder", "Don't touch the wet paint". There were notices everywhere. Louise and Miss Primty kept close to the buildings. Carriages and coaches came horribly close as they overtook each other, the horses almost snorting down Miss Primty's neck. People of all shapes and sizes and all degrees of importance were being unloaded at hotels, inns, hostelries and public houses.

'What fun it is!' exclaimed Louise. 'But I wish Douglas was here. I wonder why he didn't come?'

'Perhaps the pony needed to be shod, or something like that. He's got a long ride to-morrow with his father, remember.'

'Yes, it must be something like that,' said Louise.

But as soon as they got back to Mulberry House Louise knew something was wrong. Her mother met them at the door in a great state of anxiety.

'Douglas has disappeared,' she said. 'Your uncle has been over to see if he came here on foot as the pony is still in the field. I told him we hadn't seen him at all. They've looked everywhere.'

Louise went silent as she always did when she was troubled. She went down into the kitchen. She often found comfort there.

She stood beside baskets of fruits and vegetables, under rows of gleaming copper pans and watched silently. Pastry was being rolled and moulded on the scrubbed wooden tables. Downy feathers flew about as birds were plucked. Strong arms whisked eggs and beat wine into thick cream.

There was a knock at the back door. The sweep had called to collect the premium for Alfie who lurked in the background.

Louise's mother appeared in the kitchen. She was so concerned about Douglas that her first words to the sweep were about him.

'You went to Old College House to-day, Mr. Todd? You saw nothing of my nephew, Douglas?'

'No ma'am,' answered the sweep. 'But that place has damaged my cart. There was a hole in the ground by the coalhouse. It broke my wheel. I hope they'll pay for the damage.' But Louise's mother was too distracted to pay any attention to the sweep's complaint. She was not even interested in Alfie, the object of her charity's payment. Alfie stood looking down at the kitchen floor.

'There's a boy missing from the workhouse too,' said the sweep.

'That's strange,' said Louise's mother absently.

Louise talked to the soot-darkened child who answered in whispers of one word. He looked so miserable that Louise almost forgot her own anxiety about Douglas.

He held his arms stiffly as though his elbows hurt. He did not seem to notice the succulent aromas coming from huge bubbling iron saucepans on the gleaming, roaring range.

'Yes, ma'am. Alfie will do,' confirmed the sweep, pocketing the premium.

'You do understand, don't you Mr. Todd, that the law has forbidden you to send Alfie up the chimney?'

'Oh yes, ma'am. I know the law. All the sweeps know it. But they all use climbing boys. Except me, of course,' he added hastily.

Only then did Alfie raise his forlorn, disbelieving eyes and stare at the sweep.

'That's good,' said Louise's mother. 'He is to be your apprentice and learn your trade.'

'Certainly, ma'am,' said the sweep, getting away as fast as he could. He pushed Alfie in front of him, in case the child dared to run back and say that he had been pushed up the chimney until the skin came from his elbows and ankles, and that he had been threatened with pricks to his bare feet, and that a fire would be lighted under him if he did not hurry to get as many chimneys done as possible in a day. But Alfie was too frightened of the sweep to speak.

In the drawing room, under the bright gas chandeliers, no-one mentioned the royal visit or even the service they would all be attending in the Queen's presence the next day. They talked only of the disappearance of Douglas.

• • • • •

Meanwhile Douglas's father had given up looking for him in the open streets. He decided to search the dreadful slums of Barnwell.

'It's not fit for you to go into, sir,' said the constables who were to accompany him. But he insisted. There were criminals there. Douglas could have been kidnapped. He might have set out on foot for Mulberry House and been snatched under cover of the crowds.

The constables led the way to Barnwell. With flaming torches and loud voices of authority they went through the dark entries and along the narrow winding alleys beside the crime and grime ridden hovels. There were secret entrances where stolen goods could be brought in.

'Be careful!' said the constables. 'There are trapdoors.'

Douglas's father was shocked at what he found. 'These poor wretches,' he said, his emotions already stirred by anxiety for his son. The torches lit up gruesome corners and pathetic wrecks of humanity. 'There are children and babies in this awful place,' he said, amazed. Every now and then their grisly progress was interrupted by a blood curdling cry.

'They're cunning,' said one constable. 'Even *we* can get lost in here because they change the look of the place. They'll brick up a doorway or a window to confuse us. They're devils at it.'

'This is worse than the slums in Petty Cury,' said

Douglas's father. The wary eyes of the inhabitants flashed from the shadows. Some of the men and women reeled drunkenly in the alleyways. Others shouted at the intruders. One door refused to open at the constable's knock. Angry orders brought a slow opening of the door. The constables pushed in and in the semi-darkness the shape of a child could be made out, half hidden under a blanket, fair long curls showing at the edge of it.

'Douglas!' The constables put out their arms to steady Douglas's father as he stumbled towards the bed. But the hollow eyed young woman who had opened the door drew back the filthy coverlet.

'He's very ill,' she said, 'He's my young brother.' Shock at the sight of the emaciated boy and relief that it was not Douglas swept over Douglas's father. He groped in his pockets and handed something to the woman.

'Get a doctor,' he said, 'and medicine.' He shuddered at the idea that Douglas, so timid and delicate, might have been hidden in such a place.

• • • • •

Yet nothing in Barnwell was darker or damper than the fearful space in which at that moment, his son lay trapped. Douglas and Colley were struggling to keep awake. The candle had long ago given its last feeble flickerings.

'My father made candles. They started as long wicks and got fatter and fatter. They went in and out of the fat. They came up to set. They went up and down, up and down, over and over ...' Colley's voice failed. He dozed. Then a falling dream shook him awake. 'I like candles,' he continued, as though there had been no pause. 'They remind me of home. I asked father why the flame was dark in the middle. He didn't know.'

'It could be the angle of the wick,' suggested the future engineer drowsily, 'making a shadow.'

'My father said, "Don't look at the dark bit, look at the light round it!" I think there's nothing in the middle. It's just a dark hole ... like this one.' They both laughed and the laughter mocked their fear. The strange companionable sound ran through the tunnel under the ground. Then the total darkness took its toll of their resistance and, huddled close together, they fell deeply asleep.

CHAPTER SEVEN

Colley woke. He couldn't think where he was. His hands slid over the cold, clammy walls. Then he remembered. Douglas was ominously silent. Anxiously Colley touched him and felt the slight movement of breathing.

'Wake up, Douglas. I think it's morning,' he said, relieved that Douglas was stirring.

'Where are we?' asked Douglas, weak and confused.

'Still in the tunnel,' said Colley grimly. 'It was my idea, Douglas. I'm sorry.'

'It's not your fault. You didn't know this would happen. This must be Wednesday,' said Douglas drowsily.

'Let's write it on the wall, like the prisoners in dungeons,' said Colley. Stiff with cramp and drenched with the overnight rain, he stood up shakily. He took a piece of broken brick and scratched WEDNESDAY on the bricked up section of the tunnel.

'Wednesday. The day the Queen and Prince Consort are coming,' said Douglas in a flat voice.

'Something terrible might happen to the Queen,' said Colley.

'What do you mean?' asked Douglas, fully awake now.

'A woman told me some men were plotting something, a surprise for the Queen. I was afraid to tell the constable. I thought he was looking for me.'

'I hope we'll get out in time to warn someone,' said Douglas. Then after a silence he asked, 'How long can we go on Colley?'

'We'll go on, you'll see. We've got water anyway!' He cupped his hands and collected a small pool of rainwater. They drank it and grimaced at its acrid taste of dissolved brick.

It had been dawn when Douglas's father had returned from his all night search. Men were still working on the huge arches across Trumpington Street. He passed under the central arch and then turned in his saddle to look back. WELCOME MOST GRACIOUS SOVEREIGN and HAIL PRINCE ALBERT and GOD SAVE THE QUEEN he read. The great day had arrived, a day that no longer had anything to do with him.

Back at Old College House he sank into a chair at the dining room table and leaned forward. His head fell onto his arms but he could not sleep. Mrs. Claxton, who had waited all night, sitting in a rocking chair in her room, brought him some breakfast.

'We've searched everywhere ... except ...' he hesitated. Mrs. Claxton knew that the unspoken words were "the river".

'Don't think of that,' Mrs. Claxton comforted him. 'I last saw him with Isambard in the garden. The men are going over the grounds again. We'll find him.'

'Last night I called again at Mulberry House. They say a boy is missing from the workhouse. He disappeared the day before Douglas. Of course there couldn't be any connection, but I must go to the workhouse to-day to find out what I can.'

He set off again, riding across fen and field. As he turned towards the town, the happy cavalcade that he and Douglas should have joined, passed him with great urgency on its way to Royston. He could make no headway, so great were the crowds of horsemen and carriages, both on the road and overflowing into the fields beside it.

Going with him towards Cambridge were cartloads of jocular people pouring in from the villages, dressed in their Sunday clothes, sitting on bales of straw and clinging hilariously to the rails of overloaded wagons.

He was an outsider riding away from the general rejoicing.

At the workhouse he found no help. It was true that a boy was missing. He would return when he was hungry and then he would find himself punished.

He rode away quickly. As he reached the royal route he heard the indescribable sound of a crowd of happy people. At that moment the Queen and Prince Albert were swaying along in a closed carriage and four. Douglas's father wanted the mudsplashed outriders and the steaming horses to pass as quickly as possible. The royal carriage rolled past but for him it was like an illusion, so deeply was he engulfed in dread for the fate of his son. There was a glimpse of the young Queen smiling happily from beneath her pink bonnet. The crowd cheered and roared with pleasure, but his own voice was paralysed.

• • • • •

Later on, in King's College Chapel, Louise's thoughts were so troubled that even the arrival of the royal visitors could not console her. She wanted to enjoy the wonder of everything, to run her fingers over the velvets, silks and satins that swished, swirled, rustled and flounced around her. She wanted to touch the soft fur of the hoods hanging over scarlet and gold robes, but her small hand was clenched round the gilt fastening of her new cloak.

The chapel was a garden of huge hats and poke bonnets in full flower. Louise thought how sad the

crinkly old faces looked with their cheeks encased in bright young flowers. Pressed close to her was her mother's beaded dress. Level with her eyes pearls hung like tears round the edges of a shawl.

So many colours! They kept being broken up as her troubled eyes flitted across the scene. They were like pieces of broken glass at the bottom of her kaleidoscope constantly being shaken. She couldn't keep her thoughts still. The choirboys were singing. The Queen and the Prince followed the anthem which had been printed on white satin, edged with purple and tasselled with gold.

The young voices rose higher and higher. Louise

followed the sound up to the great roof where the
stone fans opened above her, and then to the bright
blue and red pieces of glass in the medieval windows.
Once a boy's top note had broken one of those panes.
Everything could break. The sweep's wheel had
broken ... why had it broken? Then she remember-
ed. There had been a hole near the coalhouse at Old
College House. Suddenly Louise was wide awake.
That hole. Could it have something to do with
Douglas's disappearance? Perhaps he fell through it?
She tugged at her mother's feathers.

'Mama!' she whispered, urgently, 'I've thought of
something.' Her mother turned to her in alarm and
put her finger to her lips. They were in the presence

of Her Majesty. But Louise persisted in such distress that at last her mother stooped to listen.

A message was passed to her father. He slipped out of the chapel, walking backwards in honour of the Queen. Outside, a message was given to the Commanding Officer of the troops waiting there. He gave orders to two soldiers. Immediately they moved off through the crowd and galloped off across the fen to Old College House.

CHAPTER EIGHT

Mrs. Claxton let the soldiers in.

'We've been told to search a tunnel,' they said.

'He would *never* go in there,' said Mrs. Claxton, leading them across the hall. She bent down to turn the key.

'That's strange,' she said. 'This door is unlocked. It's always kept locked.' She frowned as the soldiers went past her into the cellar with hurricane lamps.

'Is anybody there?' they shouted into the tunnel.

Douglas's father waited in a dread filled silence. Then Colley summoned all his strength. They had been found at last!

'We're here!' he called, the far away sound reaching the cellar. Hope and fear gripped Douglas's father as he sank down onto the cellar steps.

'Who is it?' the soldiers shouted.

'Douglas and Colley,' came the faint reply.

When the soldiers reached the collapsed tunnel Colley's small, strong arm was showing through the rubble. Douglas was hovering on the edge of unconsciousness from the strain of the ordeal.

'Hold on boys!' ordered the soldiers. 'We'll soon have you out.' With spades, hatchets and buckets they worked quickly to remove the earth and rubble to release the boys. Douglas was carried out and Colley staggered after him. Overwhelmed with emotion, Douglas's father took his son's limp body into his arms. But Colley shook Douglas's arm.

'Wake up, Douglas!' he cried. 'We've been found!' The tension was broken and joy burst through. Douglas revived quickly in the fresh air. Colley was almost forgotten, but after a time his shivering presence was remembered.

'Who is this boy?' asked Douglas's father.

'He's called Colley. He saved us, Papa. He made the airway. I couldn't have done it.'

'I'll be thankful to you for the rest of my life,' said the father, fervently grasping Colley's hand. Colley felt it safe to say that he had run away from the workhouse.

'He mustn't go back,' said Douglas anxiously.

'He'll never go back to that place. He'll be rewarded and so will Louise. She remembered the hole outside the coalhouse. But what on earth made you go into the tunnel when you have never even been into the cellar before?'

'Mr. Brunel,' said Douglas mysteriously and he and Colley smiled at each other through their grime.

'Did anything happen to the Queen?' asked Douglas.

'No. What could happen?'

'A woman in Falcon Yard told me that some men were planning a surprise for the Queen,' said Colley.

Douglas's father was very alarmed.

'We must send a warning at once,' he decided.

Letters were quickly written to be taken immediately, one to Mulberry House with the good news about Douglas and with enquiries about a college bedmaker to care for Colley, and the other to the officer in command of the Queen's bodyguard.

'Let's hope we are in time. This is very serious. Perhaps Her Majesty may have reason to be as grateful to you, Colley, as I am?' said Douglas's father.

The boys were given a good meal and dry clothes. Colley felt odd in Douglas's clothes with the too-long sleeves. They set off to see fireworks on Parker's Piece and the strange experience of sitting in a carriage reminded Colley of Alfie being driven away to the sweep's house. Colley himself, being small, might have been the next to go if he had not escaped. He knew that people said "climbing boys never grow up. The soot kills them." Sickening workhouse feelings came over him when he thought of Alfie.

Crowds were arriving from all directions. When the field was full of jostling folk, the fireworks began with a bang. The world burst into sparkling stars and coloured light. The gasping crowds gazed skywards as stars fell from rockets. Great flares burned with unnatural brightness. There was a great murmur of "Aah!" as the names of the Queen and Prince Albert appeared, each letter surrounded by flaming torches. Colley and Douglas looked at each other. They were thinking of the dark hole they had come from, to this bright light outside.

As the crowd dispersed, Colley caught sight of the workhouse contingent shambling along, first the boys and girls, then the women and finally the men. His heart almost stood still as he saw them, but none of the boys looked at him with his fine country clothes and grand cap covering half his face.

Then, as the men shuffled past, Jock recognised the small strange shape that was Colley. He passed quite close. Colley lifted his cap and their eyes met in the gathering darkness. Jock saw at once that Colley had fallen on his feet. He had "struck it lucky". Jock looked at him with glad surprise.

'Well done, lad,' said Jock in a low voice as he passed.

'Thanks Jock,' answered Colley. He wanted to grasp his old friend's hand, but the line had moved on.

In the town the last of the poor scholars to go home discovered the marble which had been dislodged from the ivy. He rushed to staircase Q room 2. He found Sebastian Snode dressed in his grandest attire, ruffles pouring from him at every point. Sebastian was on his way to hold silver candelabra for the Queen to inspect Newton's statue in Trinity College Chapel. He handed over the treasure and the ragged scholar sped joyfully down the stairs, his tattered gown flying over the banisters behind him.

Whilst the people had been enjoying fireworks, the university and town had been feasting and toasting the royal couple with all the magnificence their coffers could afford. Long tables almost burst their boundaries with turtle soup, succulent fish, huge barons of beef dripping with red blood and marbled with fat; the rich, dark flesh of game; the pale flesh of poultry; boars' heads and brawns following one another in a succession of courses; and all the time the wine winked and the ale frothed, whilst the poor waited for scraps outside the great kitchens.

Douglas and his father went to Mulberry House after the fireworks. Louise performed Ali Baba in her toy theatre and the drawing room was filled with joyful

clapping, more for Douglas and Louise than for Ali Baba.

Colley was given into the care of Mrs. Trundle, a warm hearted college bedmaker who lived on Castle Hill. He would stay with her and go to school again, which was what he wanted more than anything else. His journey home with her that evening took them through St. John's College grounds. As they made their way through, with other people, they were halted by a band of elegantly dressed courtiers.

'Wait!' they ordered, so Colley and Mrs Trundle stood still. Then a strangely dressed party of distinguished looking people came strolling past. Colley stared.

'It's the Queen,' whispered one of the men restraining the people. Colley put his head under the man's arm and pushed his face forward, the too-large cap being pushed to the back of his head. The Queen's jewelled tiara was still visible under the veil she had thrown over it and the skirt of her magnificent dress gave away the disguise. The Prince had hidden his evening clothes under a mackintosh.

As she passed, the Queen looked at Colley's eager face and smiled. Colley was dumbfounded. He stood stock still, even after the royal party had disappeared into the Fellows' garden.

'I've seen the Queen!' said Colley in a bemused voice as they moved on. Out on the road they were surprised by a great commotion. Soldiers were galloping about and the constables were out in force.

'What is it?' asked Mrs. Trundle of a group gathered outside an inn.

'They've caught some men, one's still on the run. There was a plot against the Queen. Thank God she's safe!'

Colley knew that he had played a part in these events but he said nothing. He was overwhelmed by the amazing things that had happened to him since he ran away from the workhouse only two days ago.

'Come on Colley,' said Mrs. Trundle. 'Let's be getting home.'

Home. It was the first time Colley had heard the word for two years.

'Thanks, Mrs Trundle,' he said and smiled. He did not think that there was anything heroic in what he had done. He only knew that he was happy and free at last.

PLACES TO VISIT IN CAMBRIDGE

1. The mill at Newnham, now a Pizza restaurant. A water wheel and the weir may be seen through a glass topped table.

2. Mill Lane, Laundress Green, Laundress Lane and Silver Street.

3. Queens' College and its wooden bridge.

4. The Senate House.

5. Great St Mary's Church with a wide view of Cambridge from the tower.

6. King's College Chapel.

7. The market square. Sebastian was right, a great fire burned nearly all the houses down not long after the Queen's visit. The rest were demolished to make the square as it is today.

8. The Red Lion outside the Central Library, symbol of all the lost inns of Petty Cury.

9. Newton's Statue in Trinity College Chapel.

10. St. John's College gardens.

11. Parker's Piece.

12. The University Botanic Garden on its new site off Trumpington Road.

13. The conduit, now at Brookside, Trumpington Road.

14. Bargees' rings still visible in the riverside college walls.

Crab Lane is now Lensfield Road.
Slaughterhouse Lane is now Corn Exchange Street.

The secret tunnel mentioned in the book is still in existence – in an old house on the outskirts of Cambridge.